To my friends and neighbors on Berkeley Place

Many thanks to Steve Aronson and Yasmin Gallop
and to the wonderful folks at Random House,
especially Janet Schulman and Erin Clarke.
—M.S.

To Josh, Ellen, and Ben
—S.R.

THIS IS A BORZOI BOOK PUBLISHED BY ALFRED A. KNOPF

Text copyright © 2004 by Marilyn Singer
Illustrations copyright © 2004 by Stephanie Roth
All rights reserved under International and Pan-American Copyright Conventions. Published in the United
States by Alfred A. Knopf, an imprint of Random House Children's Books, a division of Random House, Inc.,
New York, and simultaneously in Canada by Random House of Canada Limited, Toronto. Distributed by
Random House, Inc., New York.

KNOPF, BORZOI BOOKS, and the colophon are registered trademarks of Random House, Inc.

www.randomhouse.com/kids

Library of Congress Cataloging-in-Publication Data
Singer, Marilyn.
Block party today! / by Marilyn Singer ; illustrated by Stephanie Roth. — 1st ed.
  p. cm.
"A Borzoi Book."
SUMMARY: Three friends resolve their differences and enjoy their neighborhood's block party.
ISBN 0-375-82216-X (trade) — ISBN 0-375-92216-4 (lib. bdg.)
[1. Friendship—Fiction. 2. Parties—Fiction.] I. Roth, Stephanie, ill. II. Title.
PZ7.S6172 Bl 2004
[E]—dc21
2003001773

MANUFACTURED IN CHINA
May 2004
10 9 8 7 6 5 4 3 2 1
First Edition

TODAY!

by Marilyn Singer

illustrated by Stephanie Roth

ALFRED A. KNOPF 🐎 NEW YORK

The first Saturday in June, the sun comes up smiling
on Berkeley Place.

"Block party today." Mr. Monte hums. "Time to
sweep the sidewalk."

"Block party today." Steve and Ernie yawn. "Time to hang the banner."

"Block party today." Mercedes beams. "Time to bring out the tables and set out the grill."

"Block party today!" shout Yasmin and Sue. "No cars! No trucks! Time to run in the street! Time to play double Dutch."

"Isn't Lola going to join us?" asks Yasmin.

"Maybe, if she ever stops being mad," answers Sue.

But Lola doesn't plan to stop being mad. Ever.
She's better than they are at jump rope. She's
better—and they should have let her jump first.

She will not leave her bedroom. She will not leave her bed. "Block party today, yuck!" she grumps. "Time to stay inside all day long." She pulls the blanket over her head.

"Big fun today." Miz Watson grins, carrying out
corn bread and cookies and bright orange cake. "Time
to have a feast!"

"Big fun today," Lenny and Luis sing, rapping on their drums. "Time to play a tune."

"Big fun today." Jazzie whirls. "Time to dance to the beat."

"Big fun today!" yell Yasmin and Sue. "Jump once! Jump twice! Make it smooth. Make it nice."

"That show-off Lola's missing all the fun," says Yasmin.

"That's her fault, not ours," sniffs Sue.

But Lola's sure that they're to blame. So what if
Yasmin's got one rope! So what if Sue's got the other!
Lola's got the rhythm. Lola's got the rhyme.

She peeks through the curtain. She spies neighbors spilling out their doors, families filling up the street, and Sue and Yasmin bumping and jumping. "Big fun today, no way!" Lola scowls. "Do I have to watch those turkeys all day long?"

"Hello, summer!" The little kids giggle, lining up at
Mr. Suarez's cart. "It's snow-cone time!"

"Hello, summer!" The big kids whistle, whizzing by.
"It's rollerblading time!"

"Hello, summer!" The grown-ups slouch, fanning
their faces. "It's take-it-easy time."

"Hello, summer!" shout Yasmin and Sue. "Time to turn on the hydrant! Let's get good and wet!"

Soon they're splashing in the spray. Soon they're soaked from head to toe.

"This is fun," says Yasmin. "But I miss Lola."
"Yeah, I do, too," says Sue. "Maybe we should go get her."
They turn around, and there she is, sitting on her stoop,
trying to glare. But she looks more sad than mad.

She gets up slowly and takes two tiny steps their
way. And before she can say, "Hello, summer!" Yasmin
and Sue pull her under the spray. First Lola squeals.
Then Lola laughs. She splashes her friends. They splash
her right back. Soon they link arms and squish down
the street.

When it's time again for double Dutch, Yasmin and
Sue let Lola go first. But by then she doesn't care.

Later, they sit on Lola's stoop, close as three baby
sparrows hatching under Mr. Monte's roof.

"Block party today," says Yasmin. "Wasn't it stupendous?"

"Block party today," says Sue. "Wasn't it great?"

"Block party today, ha!" Lola growls. "It wasn't stupendous. It wasn't even great."

"Huh?" Yasmin and Sue gasp.

Then Lola grins a wicked grin. "Block party today! It was the best!"

Yasmin and Sue grin, too. And three good friends settle back to watch the sun sink, smiling softly, on Berkeley Place on the first Saturday in June.